SECRETS OF AN OVER SURVIVOR

THE WITCH'S WARNING

GREYSON MANN

ILLUSTRATED BY GRACE SANDFORD

Sky Pony Press
New York

Copyright © 2017 by Hollan Publishing, Inc.

Minecraft® is a registered trademark of Notch Development AB.

The Minecraft game is copyright © Mojang AB.

Sky Pony Press books may be purchased in bulk at special discounts for sales promotion, corporate gifts, fund-raising, or educational purposes. Special editions can also be created to specifications. For details, contact the Special Sales Department, Sky Pony Press, 307 West 36th Street, 11th Floor, New York, NY 10018 or info@skyhorsepublishing.com.

Sky Pony® is a registered trademark of Skyhorse Publishing, Inc.®, a Delaware corporation.

Minecraft® is a registered trademark of Notch Development AB.
The Minecraft game is copyright © Mojang AB.

Visit our website at www.skyponypress.com.

10 9 8 7 6 5 4 3 2

Library of Congress Cataloging-in-Publication Data is available on file.

Special thanks to Erin L. Falligant.

Cover illustration by Grace Sandford
Cover design by Brian Peterson

Paperback ISBN: 978-1-5107-2707-6
EBook ISBN: 978-1-5107-2712-0

Printed in Canada

Interior design by Joshua Barnaby

CHAPTER 1

"Fire! Take cover!"

Will ducked, as if dodging flames.

From the brewing stand in the corner of the room, Mina grinned. "We're not making fire," she said. "We're making potion of fire *resistance*. Now get back here, would you?"

Will faked fear as he tiptoed toward the brewing stand. "Well, there's sure a whole lot of smoke." The gray haze filled the room, curling up from the blaze rod in the center of the stand. Will pretended to cough—until he saw Mina plunk a few Nether wart buds into a glass water bottle.

"Is that from Seth's garden?"

She nodded. "I can't believe he grew Nether wart in a greenhouse. No more trips to the Nether!"

What? No more trips to the Nether meant no more battles with ghasts or wither skeletons. Will was about to protest when he noticed the potion on the brewing stand bubbling.

"Something's happening!" he cried. "Is that the potion of fire resistance?"

Mina shook her head. "We made awkward potion. That's only the first step. Could you please hand me the magma cream?"

Will reached for the glistening-wet ball on the crafting table. It looked like slime, except the green mass was streaked with red and yellow swirls. Was that from the blaze powder Mina had mixed in?

"Whoops!" Will pretended to let the magma cream slip through his fingers and then caught it again.

"Don't drop that!" said Mina, her eyes wide. "This is serious business.

We're going to need these potions when it comes time for battle."

Will patted his side. "Not if I have my trusty sword." He really, *really* hoped Mina would be done brewing soon. His whole body was itching to get outside and take on a mob or two.

"There's more than one way to fight a battle, Will," said Mina thoughtfully as she slid the slippery magma cream into the awkward potion.

When the liquid popped and fizzled, Will stepped closer. Orange bubbles drifted up and out of the glass bottle. Just as he reached out to touch one—

Crack!

A deafening sound split the room.

This time, Will ducked for real.
"Yikes! Was that the potion?" His
wolf-dog, Buddy, whined from her
bed in the corner.

"No. Lightning, I think," Mina
whispered, giggling. "But we're safe in
here. Your brother's house is rock solid."

"That's right!" Will's big brother,
Seth, stepped into the room. He

knocked on the stone wall with his knuckles. "Solid obsidian. So what are you two brewing?"

"Potion of fire resistance," Will announced. "Ta-da!"

"Awesome!" said Seth. "Now if you could just brew me up a potion

of lightning resistance, I could head outside and feed the animals some breakfast."

Will turned to Mina. "Is that a real potion?"

She shook her head. "But I wish it were. Is it ever going to stop raining in Little Oak?"

Seth let out an enormous sigh, his frustration bubbling over like potion from a bottle. "My fields are totally swamped with water."

That reminded Will of something. "Hey, I heard a story in town about witches, like the kind that live in the swamp. Did you know that lightning can turn villagers into witches?"

"That's not true," said Mina as she lifted the potion of fire resistance up to the light.

Seth shrugged. "It *could* be true, I guess. Lightning super-charges creepers. And it can turn pigs into zombie pigmen. So . . . who knows?"

Will shot his brother a grateful smile.

"Well, here's what I *know* is true," said Mina, searching her crafting table. "I'm running low on potion ingredients. As soon as the storm passes, I'm heading into town for more—and stopping by the swamp for some slime."

"I'm going, too!" said Will, jumping up and reaching for his sword. Finally, something was actually happening around here!

Buddy lifted her head and whined. When it came time for adventure, she didn't like to be left behind.

But as another crack of lightning lit up the brewing room, Will slid his sword back into his sheath.

It wasn't time for adventure just *yet*.
He sighed and turned back toward the
brewing stand.

"There's one!" whispered Mina. She
pulled Will behind the trunk of an
oak tree. "Do you see it?"

He narrowed his eyes and gazed across
the swamp. He could barely see the
outline of the house through the gently
falling rain. It looked like a tree house
built on stilts. "That's a witch hut?"

"It sure is." Mina wrung the water
from her long red ponytail. "And this is
about as close to one as I want to get."

Will scoffed. "What do you mean? With your potions, you could take on a witch *any* day."

But Mina didn't seem so sure. "They brew even more powerful potions," she murmured. "And they know how to use them."

Was she speaking from experience? Will wanted to ask her. But through the sound of the rain plopping onto the soggy ground, he heard something else.

Squish, slop, squish, slop, squish, slop . . .

Something was coming closer.

Something wet.

Something slimy.

And something very, *very* large.

CHAPTER 2

Splat!

The giant slime hit Will from behind and knocked him to the ground.

He slipped and scrambled in the mud, trying to get his footing, just as Mina slashed at the slime with her sword.

Three or four smaller slime scattered across the ground. *Squish, slop, squish, slop, squish, slop . . .*

As the bouncing mobs circled around
Will, he pulled his sword from his side.
But before he could strike, a streak of
gray fur darted in front of him.

Buddy!

She snapped her jaws around a mini
slime and shook her head until the
slime burst. Gooey green globs fell

from Buddy's muzzle, bouncing onto the ground below. Then she crouched low, ready to attack again.

"No! Don't let her eat them!" cried Mina. "We need the slime balls for magma cream!"

"She's not *eating* them," said Will. "She's killing them. She's helping us!"

But as Buddy swallowed the next slime whole and licked the green ooze off her muzzle, Will cleared his throat, hoping Mina hadn't seen.

"Buddy. Sit!"

The dog whined, but she obeyed.

Squish, squish, slop, squish, squish, slop . . .

Mini slimes were everywhere now.

With each strike of his sword, Will created more gooey little mobs. They stuck to his pant legs and squished under his feet.

Finally, nothing was left but a moss-green carpet of sticky slime balls.

"Yes!" Mina pulled out her sack. "Help me pick them up."

Will grabbed them by the handful, shaking his fingers to force the gooey balls to fall into the sack. "Ick."

When Mina wasn't looking, he let Buddy lick his fingers clean. Then he glanced back at the witch huts in the distance.

Slime were too easy to kill. When would the *real* battles begin? He stared at the door of one witch hut, willing a witch to come out. But it didn't open—not even a crack. And Mina was already heading down the trail toward town.

By the time Will and Mina had finished trading with villagers in Little Oak, storm clouds were brewing again.

"What did you get?" Will asked as they hurried across the courtyard.

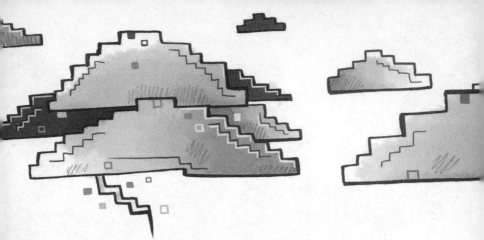

Mina rattled off her trades on
her fingertips. "Pufferfish from the
fisherman—good for potion of water
breathing. Gunpowder from the miner
to make splash potions. Redstone
from the priest for extended potions.
And . . . what was the last one?" She
tapped her finger on her chin. "Sugar!
For potion of swiftness."

As thunder rumbled overhead,
Will checked the sky. "Do you think

any mobs will spawn? It's so dark out today!"

Mina shrugged. "I'm not thinking about mobs. I'm thinking about books. I need to check out a book from the library. C'mon!"

Will made Buddy sit in front of the stone building. Librarian Wick had a strict "no dogs allowed" policy. She had even posted a warning sign:

So Buddy lowered herself onto her belly with a sigh and rested her chin on her paws.

Then Will followed Mina up the creaky steps and onto the dimly lit main floor. Bookshelves filled with colorful, leather-bound books marched in tidy rows from the front of the library to the back.

As Mina turned down an aisle of books, she ran her finger across the spines. "Ooh, this looks new." She slid a thin leather-bound book from the shelf and showed Will the red cover. He had to squint to read it in the darkness: *Advanced Potions for Master Brewers*.

"Sounds about right," he said. He was pretty sure Mina could *write* a book on brewing by now.

She set the book down on the checkout counter next to Jack o' Lantern, the librarian's orange tabby cat. "Hi, Jacko." The three-legged cat purred as Mina stroked his head.

But when Will reached out his hand, the hair on Jacko's back stood up. Will stepped backward. "Sorry. I probably smell like wolf."

Everyone in Little Oak knew that Jacko had lost his leg in a battle with a wolf. So even though Will had tamed Buddy long ago, *all* dogs smelled like "wolf" to Jacko.

"Ms. Wick?" Mina called. Her voice bounced off the high walls and ceiling. "She's never at her desk."

"I know. I'm pretty sure she likes books more than people," Will joked. Together, they began searching the shadowy walkways between the bookshelves.

Sure enough, they found the white-haired librarian sitting on the floor like a villager child, reading a thick book with yellowed pages.

"Ms. Wick?" Mina whispered.

The woman didn't budge.

"Ms. Wick?"

"Oh!" The librarian jumped up, nearly dropping her book. "My goodness. Will and Mina. What are you doing here?"

Mina raised an eyebrow. "Um . . . checking out a book?" She hid her smile. "I'd like this one on potion brewing."

Ms. Wick adjusted her glasses and studied the book in Mina's hand. "Oh, yes, that's a good one. A very good one, indeed." She held the book as if it were a baby and then squeezed it to her chest. "But I'm afraid I'm reading that one right now. Let me find you another one, dear." As they passed the checkout counter, she placed the red book on a teetering pile marked, "Reserved."

Will caught Mina's eye and grinned. Ms. Wick's books *were* her babies!

Suddenly, a clap of thunder rattled the walls of the library.

Yeeeowl!

Jacko flew off the counter and darted in front of Will. At the same time, the front door to the library swung open. As a brown-robed farmer stepped inside, the tabby cat made a beeline for the doorway.

"Jacko! No!" Ms. Wick tore after the cat, nearly tripping over her robes.

When Jacko hit the front stoop, he crouched low in the rain. Ms. Wick scooped him up in her arms just as the lightning bolt struck.

In the light cast by the brilliant, jagged streak, Will saw Ms. Wick's white hair stand straight up.

And then she was gone.

And a white-haired witch stood in her place, holding a *very* freaked-out tabby cat.

CHAPTER 3

"Ms. Wick!"

Will and Mina hit the doorway at the same time, squeezing past each other to get out onto the stoop.

But Ms. Wick was gone.

And now the *witch* was, too.

Buddy bounded up the staircase toward Will, stopping to sniff each step.

"Did you . . . see that?" asked Will. He rubbed his eyes, wondering if the lightning had played tricks on him.

"Y-yes," said Mina in a wobbly voice. "But I don't believe it."

"See what?" asked the farmer, scratching his head.

"Um, nothing," said Mina, giving Will the look that meant "stay quiet."

They waited until the farmer had gone into the library before speaking again.

"I told you!" Will couldn't help saying. "Lightning can turn villagers into witches!"

"That's ridiculous," said Mina, starting to sound more like her old self. "She's around here somewhere. Ms. Wick!"

Mina shaded her eyes from the rain and searched the gloomy courtyard. Buddy searched, too, nosing the gravel around the base of the steps. She *woofed* and wagged her tail.

"Buddy found something!" said Will.

He crouched near the dog, trying to see what Buddy saw. But the dark clouds overhead crowded out what little daylight was left.

"Here," said Mina, pulling a torch from her sack and lighting it.

In the flickering light, they could make out paw prints. "Cat prints?" asked Mina.

"I think so," said Will. As he followed the tidy path of prints, he noticed a pattern—two prints, and then one, two prints, and then one. He sucked in his breath. "It's a three-legged cat. It's Jacko. Let's go!"

But even with Buddy in the lead, Will and Mina couldn't catch up with Jacko. The cat's trail led them through the courtyard of Little Oak, past the cobblestone well, and right out the other side of town.

When they couldn't see the paw prints anymore, Buddy led the way, following her nose.

And soon enough, Will
knew exactly where
they were going.

Mina did, too.

She turned toward him, her green
eyes wide, and mouthed the words.
"The swamp."

As Will slogged toward the swamp,
trying to keep up with Buddy, wetness
seeped into his shoes.

In the shadows ahead, he saw nothing.
He tripped over vines and dodged sugar
cane as if the tall stalks were skeletons
preparing to pelt him with arrows.

"Ms. Wick!" Mina's voice rang out again.

Will was glad to hear Mina's voice behind him. But no one answered.

Then, as the sky lit up with lightning, he saw her up ahead.

Ms. Wick.

Witch Wick, her long white hair flowing out from beneath her black hat. She held Jacko tightly in her arms, and the cat's eyes glowed yellow in the darkness.

Buddy saw them, too. As the dog growled and lunged forward, Jacko sprang from the witch's arms.

Fear and anger rolled across the witch's face like storm clouds. In an

instant, she held a potion in her hand. Glass shattered. And Buddy yelped.

"No! Buddy!" Will ran toward the whimper. "Where are you?"

He nearly tripped over the dog, who stood still as a statue in the tall grass.

"What's wrong? Are you hurt?"

Mina was suddenly beside them with her torch. She held the light up as Buddy took a slow step forward. And then another. "Potion of slowness," Mina said. "She's not hurt. Just scared."

"She can't move?" Will wanted to lift the dog in his arms, but Buddy was too heavy. She looked up at him with dark, fearful eyes and whimpered again.

"It'll pass," said Mina. "Let's wait with her." She squatted beside Buddy on the wet ground.

But Will's sword was already in his hand. "You wait," he said. "I've got a witch to battle."

"Will, no!" Mina reached up to grab his arm. "It's Librarian Wick!"

Will yanked his arm away. "She's *Witch* Wick now. And she hurt Buddy!"

"Only because she thought he was going to hurt her cat," Mina said quickly. "Think about it. She could have thrown a potion of harming at *you*. Or at me. But she didn't. She just slowed Buddy down a little.

Remember, Will. There's more than one way to fight a battle."

Will tried to swallow his anger, but it raged inside like the storm overhead. Only when Buddy could walk again, *really* walk, did Will feel his insides start to quiet.

"C'mon," said Mina. "Let's put Buddy on a leash and see if we can find the trail again."

Will fished a lead rope from out from his sack and tied it around Buddy's collar. Usually, Buddy strained at the leash, trying to break free. But now, she seemed content to walk behind Will rather than out in front.

"You're still spooked, aren't you, girl?" he asked, reaching down to scratch her head.

He couldn't blame her.

Any mob could spawn at any time in this dark swamp.

As he straightened back up, Mina whirled around in front of him. She hollered something, her eyes wide with fear.

What had she said?

Will heard nothing—except the *crash* of a potion bottle at his feet.

CHAPTER 4

Will felt the effects of the poison before he saw the witch who had thrown it. His stomach turned, and his legs wobbled beneath him.

Then someone yanked him sideways, and he fell into a cluster of vines.

"Lie down," Mina ordered.

"Wait! Where's Buddy?"

A wet lick across his face told Will that his dog had followed him into hiding.

"Drink this," said Mina, propping Will's head up in her hand.

He didn't ask what he was drinking. He had learned a long time ago not to ask about Mina's potions. They were usually made with something disgusting, like ghast tears or spider eyes. But they *also* usually worked.

He was surprised to taste sweet melon.

"Potion of healing," said Mina. "But don't drink too much. I have a feeling we're going to need a lot more of this."

She capped off the bottle as Will propped himself up on his elbows.

Slowly, the room stopped spinning.

"Was it Witch Wick?" he asked.

"No," said Mina. "Three new witches spawned—none of them Librarian Wick. That means it's okay to fight them."

Buddy growled, as if to say, "Me, too."

When Will felt strong enough to sit up, Mina peeked through the vines. "So we need to stay as far away from the witches as we can. Climb a tree and get up high. Stay out of range of their potions and then hit them as hard as you can with your bow and arrow—*fast*, before they can drink potions of healing. Got it?"

"I'm better with my sword," said Will, patting the handle.

Mina shook her head. "You can't get that close."

Before Will could argue, she was gone, stepping through the vines.

When he heard a glass potion bottle smash to smithereens, he sprang to his feet and darted out after her.

Mina raced *away* from the witches, her bow and arrow drawn. So Will followed her and then veered left, scrambling up a spruce tree.

The branches were wet and slippery, but at least they were close together. He climbed easily toward the top.

A *yelp* from down below reminded him that Buddy *couldn't* climb the tree.

"Sit!" ordered Will. "Stay!"

Buddy dropped her rump obediently. But when Will released his first arrow, she took off running. She wanted to protect him and do her part.

"Buddy, no!"

Will watched helplessly as the dog bounded toward one of the witches, dodging her splash potions and lunging at her arm. Buddy bit down hard—Will

could tell by
the witch's
cry. She toppled
backward.

Now it was time
for Will to do *his*
part. He placed
another arrow
in the bow,
pulled back,
and released.
Thwang! The arrow
sailed through the trees and hit its mark—
the second witch, who stood a few yards
away from the first.

"Gotcha!" cried Will, pumping his
fist.

But there was no time to celebrate. As soon as the arrow hit, the witch guzzled her potion of healing. Bubbles floated upward toward Will's hiding place in the spruce.

So he shot another arrow. And another. And another.

More arrows sailed through the trees from over his shoulder. Mina was fighting from the top of another tree.

Finally, the second witch toppled. And Buddy was back, fighting the third.

"Buddy, no!" Will cried. How could he shoot the witch with arrows if Buddy was in the way?

There was nothing to do now but wait and hope that Buddy was strong enough. Fast enough. Fierce enough.

Will heard the shatter of glass and knew Buddy had been hit by *something*. But she wouldn't quit. She attacked the witch again and again, pushing her back toward the swamp. And finally, with a grunt, the witch dropped.

"Buddy!"

Will slid down the trunk of the tree, breaking small branches and scratching his arms and legs. By the time he hit the ground, Mina was already running.

When they got to Buddy, the dog was panting and lying on her side—but awake.

"Give her this," said Mina, shoving the potion of healing into Will's hand. "She'll take it from you."

He dribbled a bit of the potion into Buddy's mouth, but it ran out the other side. He was relieved when Buddy lapped it off her muzzle with her tongue.

While he waited beside her, gently stroking her fur, Mina collected the drops the witches had left behind: spider eyes, gunpowder, and redstone.

"Ooh, glowstone dust," she said, scooping up the fine red powder. "We can use this to make more potions of healing."

By the time Mina had collected the last drop—a stick of some sort—Buddy was well enough to grab it out of her hand and promptly start to chew on it.

Mina laughed. "She's feeling better! That's a good sign."

But Will had his eyes trained on something else.

"Look," he whispered, pointing toward the witch hut in the distance.

A witch stood on the porch, watching them.

"Ms. Wick!" cried Mina, jumping to her feet.

But as soon as the witch heard Mina's voice, she hurried down the ladder toward the swamp, her long white hair flowing behind her.

"Oh, poor Ms. Wick," said Mina with a sigh. "How can we help her?"

"I don't know," Will mumbled. He wasn't sure he *wanted* to help Witch Wick, not after what she had done to Buddy. In fact, right now, he kind of just wanted to head home—to dry off and make sure Buddy was okay.

Until he heard what Mina had to say next.

"Have you ever been inside a witch hut?"

CHAPTER 5

"We can't touch anything," said Mina. "We're just looking—to see if there's something in there we can use to help Ms. Wick."

"I know," said Will as he climbed the ladder behind her. With every step, he turned back toward shore to make sure Buddy was okay. "I can't see her!" he said again.

"Of course you can't," said Mina. "That's the whole point of potion of invisibility."

Buddy was somewhere on shore, tied to a tree. Will had watched her lap up Mina's potion of invisibility, made with fermented spider eye. He shivered, remembering the smell.

And then? That furry wolf-dog had slowly disappeared.

Will had still been able to hear her panting and feel her wet tongue on his hand. But he couldn't *see* her. Which meant witches and other mobs couldn't either.

"She's safer there than up here," said Mina. "Besides, if we run into Jacko, we won't want Buddy with us."

True, thought Will. He was surprised Witch Wick hadn't posted a warning sign on her hut: "Dogs Beware."

As soon as Will stepped off the ladder onto the deck, a shiver ran down his spine. He wasn't sure he and Mina should be trespassing in this witch hut either. *Are we really going inside?*

The deck creaked beneath his feet as he followed Mina toward the door. It was slightly ajar, and Mina peeked through the crack before stepping through it.

Will held his breath as he followed her in. As rain pitter-pattered overhead, he took in the contents of the hut: A cauldron and crafting table. A pot filled with mushrooms. A shelf lined with potion ingredients. And a book—a very familiar book with a red leather cover—resting beside the glass jars.

Mina saw it, too, and reached out to touch the embossed cover. *Advanced Potions for Master Brewers.*

"I guess Witch Wick—I mean, Librarian Wick—needs the book now more than I do," she murmured.

Will nodded. "I just hope she doesn't use any of those potions on *us.*"

Mina made a face. "She *won't,* Will. She doesn't want to hurt us—I told you that! She only used the potion on Buddy to protect Jacko."

As soon as she said the cat's name, they heard a pitiful meow. From behind the cauldron, Jacko wound his way into the room, right toward Will.

"Oh, are we friends now?" asked Will, squatting and holding out his hand.

The cat butted his head against Will's fingers and then meowed again, as if to say, "What in the Overworld is going on? And when are we going back to the library?"

"Poor Jacko," said Mina, dropping to the floor beside him. "We have to figure out a way to save Ms. Wick, to make her human again."

As Will slowly stroked Jacko's back and tail, he imagined what it would be like if he couldn't be with Buddy. Or if Buddy couldn't be with *him*. Finally, he nodded. "Okay. I'm in."

Mina's face lit up. "Good," she said. "We'll go back to the library tomorrow and do some research. There has to be a way to help Ms. Wick. There *has* to!"

By the time Will and Mina made it back to shore, Buddy's potion of invisibility was wearing off—sort of. Her head, tail, and paws were visible. But the rest of her wasn't.

She chased her "floating" tail in circles for a while, as if it belonged to another dog. But when Will whistled for her, she barked and raced past him, leading the way toward home.

As soon as they reached the farm, Will knew something was wrong. But what?

The garden was black with mud—that was nothing new, after a solid week of rain. And he could hear the pigs grunting in the shed. Buddy raced over to sniff at the door.

But something was different.

Though night had fallen and the clouds were thick overhead, the farm was bathed in an eerie purple glow.

"Is that . . . a Nether portal?" asked Mina as she rounded the shed.

Will raced after her and stopped to stare at the obsidian frame built on the hillside. Purple flames flickered inside.

He knew Seth would never go through it alone—not without Mina's potion of fire resistance. *Not without me to protect him,* thought Will. *Right?*

"Seth!" He raced toward the house, hoping his brother was inside.

Just then, the garden gate popped open and Seth burst out.

Relief flooded Will's chest. But as Seth glanced over his shoulder, Will realized his brother wasn't running

toward him. He was running *away* from something else. But what?

Will heard a grunt from the garden. And then an angry squeal. Was it a pig?

As the mob came into view, pink as a pig but tall as a zombie—and much, *much* faster—Will knew exactly what was chasing his brother.

A zombie pigman.

CHAPTER 6

Seth tore past Will toward the Nether portal.

For a split second, Will feared his brother would dive into the purple flames headfirst, straight into the lava pools on the other side of that portal. "Seth, stop!"

He charged after the zombie pigman just as Seth rounded the corner of the portal. He *hadn't* gone through.

But the zombie pigman was veering around the portal, too. He was right on Seth's heels.

Will raced around the portal from the other side. He nearly ran smack into Seth, who suddenly tripped and started rolling down the muddy hillside. Then Will stood face to face with the snarling zombie pigman.

As the pigman raised his sword, Will did, too. He knocked the pigman back a step. Then sideways. If he could keep pushing him back, toward the portal, *maybe* he could force him right through.

"Don't hurt him!" cried Seth from the hillside below. "That's my pig!"

What? thought Will. *Your pig?*

With one more blow of his sword, the pigman toppled through the portal. He disappeared with a squeal and a flash of purple smoke.

"Your pig?" asked Will again as he hurried down the hill to help Seth back up.

"Yes!" said Seth, out of breath. "Lightning hit a few of my pigs and turned them into zombie pigmen. I didn't want to hurt him!"

"He's not hurt," said Mina, reaching out her hand toward Seth, too. "Thanks to Will, he's back in the Nether, where zombie pigmen belong."

Seth nodded, but he looked so sad. "Some of the others wandered away already," he said.

"Is there a way to turn them back into pigs?" asked Will.

Seth shook his head. "The lightning did its damage."

Will and Mina locked eyes. "It's done a lot of damage," Will said quietly. He wanted to tell Seth about Librarian Wick, but he couldn't yet. Not when Seth was still so sad about his pigs.

He couldn't save his pigs, thought Will as Seth extinguished the flames of the portal. *Will we be able to save Ms. Wick?*

Thunder rumbled overhead. Yes, the lightning had done its damage. And it wasn't done yet.

Seth was gone by morning, in search of his wandering zombie pigmen. So Will and Mina set off for Little Oak, hoping the library would hold the clues to saving Ms. Wick.

It was raining. *Still.* Buddy loped ahead down the trail, biting at raindrops in the air as if she was ready for the rain to end, too.

Suddenly, the dog stopped in her tracks. Her ears tilted forward. She let out a low growl and then took off— not toward Little Oak, but toward the swamp.

"Buddy!"

Will raced after her, remembering how the dog had been struck down by the witch's potion just yesterday.

He hadn't even reached the swamp before he heard the sounds of battle.

As he hid behind a mass of vines, Mina came up behind him.

"What is it?" she asked. "Which mobs?"

Will listened. He heard the blast of a creeper. The *thwang* of arrows. The grunts and groans of zombies. "I don't know," he whispered, his mouth suddenly dry. "A lot of them."

Then he heard the *yelp* of a wolf-dog. And he charged full steam ahead.

Beneath the dark, stormy skies, the swamp had become a battleground. It teemed with mobs that had spawned overnight—skeletons and zombies that hadn't burned up in the morning light, because sunlight had never come!

Will reached immediately for his bow and arrow. Like witches, skeletons were best battled from a distance.

But where was Buddy?

Thwang!

As a skeleton's arrow sailed overhead, Will ducked. He launched an arrow of his own and whirled around just in time to dodge a staggering zombie. Dropping his bow and arrow, Will grabbed his sword and lunged at the zombie, knocking him back.

Another arrow *zinged* through the air, just above his ear.

"Will, c'mon! We gotta get to the water!" Mina raced past him into the swamp.

Will took one last look for Buddy. Then he followed Mina across a lily pad bridge, feeling the cool swamp water soak through his shoes. Soon they were climbing the ladder to a witch hut.

"Is there a witch inside?" Will called up to Mina.

Her voice sounded muffled. "I don't know. But it's safer here in the swamp than onshore. Most mobs take damage from water."

As a crack of lightning split the sky, Will didn't feel so safe. But he followed Mina up to the deck of the hut. Then he heard the crash of glass. *Uh-oh. Witch alert.*

Another crash from a nearby hut caught his ear—and his eye. "Mina!" he cried. "The witches are battling *each other.*"

A witch in dark robes guzzled a potion of healing while the witch at the hut next to hers prepared to launch another potion.

"What's happening?" asked Will as thunder rumbled overhead. "Has the whole Overworld gone crazy?"

Mina set her jaw. "I don't know. But Ms. Wick isn't safe here. We have to get to the library and figure out how to turn her back!" She pulled something out of her sack—a glass vial filled with golden yellow liquid. "Potion of water breathing. If we drink this, we can swim to shore underwater and then get back to Little Oak." She unscrewed the lid and began to drink.

"But I can't go yet," Will said suddenly. "I don't even know where Buddy is!" He scanned the shoreline, hoping to see his furry friend bounding through the water.

But Mina had already swallowed the potion. "I don't have much time," she said. "Here, take this." She handed Will her sack of potions and climbed down the ladder. "I'll be back!"

From the deck above, Will watched until she reached the bottom rung— just as another bolt of lightning struck.

It streaked across the sky, top to bottom.

It hit the base of the ladder, which burst into flames.

And then it faded into darkness.

Taking Mina with it.

CHAPTER 7

"Mina!"

As flames crept up the ladder, Will tried not to panic. "She's okay," he told himself. "She's okay."

But how could she be? And where was she?

The heat from the fire forced him to the other side of the deck. He glanced wildly down at the water and then back up at the shoreline, which seemed awfully far way.

The empty deck of the hut next door was closer. Close enough to jump to? Could he throw a rope or Buddy's leash and swing over?

Maybe. But suddenly, that deck wasn't empty anymore.

A witch appeared, staring at Will with cold, dark eyes.

A witch with a wiggly, warty nose.

And a big black hat.

And *very* red hair.

"Mina?" Will's voice came out so quietly, he wasn't sure he'd spoken at all. A wave of dread threatened to wash him right over the deck rail.

Don't panic, he told himself again.

If that *was* Mina, maybe she would help him.

He forced himself to look up, hoping to find his friend somewhere in that witch's scowling face. Instead, he found an enemy.

The witch's arm snapped forward. A bottle of potion hurtled through the air toward Will as if in slow motion. As it struck the deck beside Will, he made up his mind. *I won't fight Mina. I won't.*

He grabbed the sack Mina had given him and jumped over the railing into the swirling swamp below.

The cold water took his breath away. As he sank into the murky water, he could barely see his hand in front of his face. His feet struck soft bottom.

Swim, he ordered himself. *Swim!*

So he did, not sure where he was going or where he would end up.

When he bumped into a ladder, he grabbed it and held tight. Then he waited underwater until his lungs felt as if they would burst.

Finally, he broke the surface of the water, gulping at the cool air.

He looked up, wondering which hut he'd stumbled upon. It wasn't on fire. And the deck seemed empty. But was it?

He climbed slowly until his eyes were just above the rim of the deck. Then he glanced in both directions, and breathed a sigh of relief.

No witches. No Mina. No Librarian Wick.

He sprawled out on the deck and quickly dumped out the contents of Mina's sack.

Glass bottles clinked together, their colorful contents sloshing inside. But without his friend, he didn't know which potion was which. How could he save her? How could he even defend himself?

When the bubble of a potion floated into view, Will stared at it in confusion. Had it come from one of his bottles? No—he hadn't opened one yet!

He looked up just in time to see the redheaded witch round the corner of the deck. She furrowed her brow and reached for a potion.

Will moved with lightning-quick speed, as if he'd just sucked down a potion of swiftness. Without thinking, he grabbed the sack and raced around the other side of the deck. Then he remembered Mina's words. *Get up high.*

Could he climb onto the roof of the hut? He had to try.

His feet slipped on the wet boards, but he pulled himself upward using the last of his strength. Then he lay on his stomach, peering just over the edge of the roof.

Down below, Mina the Witch studied him with beady purple eyes. She tossed a potion, which shattered against the wall of the hut. She threw another. This one landed on the roof and rolled off without breaking.

Will fingered his bow and arrow. From up here, he could easily shoot her. *But I won't,* he thought again. *I won't fight Mina!*

As the witch launched another bottle, Will heard breaking glass and smelled something foul. Then he felt the familiar churning in his stomach. He'd been poisoned. By Mina. His best friend!

And he had no idea what to do.

As the world began to spin, he held on tightly to the roof with one arm and dug into the sack with the other.

It smells like melon, he remembered. *The potion I need smells like melon!*

But he couldn't remember the color. And he couldn't open the bottles to sniff them, not with one hand. Not when his arms felt . . . so . . . heavy.

As his eyelids began to close, something drifted into view. Something red and leather bound. It fluttered open and landed on his chest with a *thud*.

Ms. Wick's book of potions?

He lifted his head just enough to read the open page. *Potion of healing.* The image showed a glass bottle with red liquid, a potion as red as the cover of the book resting on his chest.

Will fumbled through the bag, lifting vials until he found it—the red one that tasted like melon. He untwisted the cap and poured it into his mouth, half drinking and half choking it down.

Then he lay back and closed his eyes.

"Will, shoot her! Fight!"

He woke to the sound of Mina screaming from down below.

As he rolled onto his side and glanced down, he saw why. The redheaded witch was tossing potions, bottle after bottle, at Mina. Bubbles rose as Mina fell. *Mina* fell.

His friend.

His redheaded friend!

So . . . who was the witch attacking her?

CHAPTER 8

"Mina!"

Will's head felt thick and foggy. There was no time to think. Only time to act.

He grabbed the bow at his side and fired arrows, one after another, at the witch. Each time she reached for her potion of healing, he cut her off with another arrow. She staggered backward.

With one last arrow, he sent her over the rail and flailing toward the swamp water below.

"Mina!"

Will slipped and slid over the edge of the roof and dropped down to the deck, his sack in tow. He knelt beside Mina, whose face was pale and cold.

"I don't know what to do!" he cried.

And then he remembered. He *did* know what to do.

He pulled out the potion of healing, which still held a few drops of precious liquid, and dribbled it into Mina's mouth. But he needed more. Of what?

He flipped frantically through Ms. Wick's book on potion brewing until he reached the section on healing potions.

There! A purple potion of regeneration. Did Mina have it in her sack?

He poured out the glass vials, hoping they wouldn't break. When he saw a bottle of purple potion glimmering from the bottom of the pile, he felt a rush of hope. "Yes!"

He opened the vial and lifted Mina's head so that she could drink.

She guzzled the liquid like one of the baby lambs on Seth's farm. Slowly, her cheeks turned pink again. And she opened her eyes wide.

"The witch!" she said, her voice raspy. "Why weren't you fighting her? I thought we were going to die!"

Will felt his own cheeks redden. "Because . . . I thought she was *you*," he admitted. "You were struck by lightning! I thought you turned into a witch!"

Mina laughed weakly. "No," she said. "I was already underwater. I was safe." Then she propped herself up on her elbows. "So you were just going to let her kill you? Because you thought she was me?"

She stared at Will with such wonder that he had to look away.

He puffed out his chest. "Nah, I wasn't going to let her kill me. I was just dodging her attacks. There's more than *one* way to fight a battle, you know."

Mina shook her head and smiled. "You're right. That's true."

Then Will remembered something. "And . . . I had help." He showed Mina the book. "Ms. Wick got it to me, *somehow,* right when I needed it most!"

As he described how the book had "arrived," Mina sat straight up. "Potion of invisibility?" she said. "She brought it to you! I told you she didn't want to hurt you!"

Will nodded. "Can we help her, too? Did you find anything at the library?"

Mina shook her head sadly. "No," she said softly. "There's no cure."

Will slumped down beside her and rested his head against the wall. "Well, at least we know she can protect herself," he said. "She knows how to use potions—that's a good start. Remember how she used that potion on Buddy?"

Mina whimpered beside him.

Except, it *wasn't* Mina.

"Buddy?"

A loud *woof* sounded from the other side of the wall.

"She's inside!" shouted Will, jumping up and racing for the door. He drew his sword, in case there was a witch in the hut. Then he barreled through the door to save his dog.

But Buddy was alone in the hut—in *Ms. Wick's hut.* Will recognized it from the last time!

Buddy barked again and greeted Will with a sloppy kiss on the chin. She didn't seem to be hurt. So what was she doing in here?

Mina must have been wondering the same thing. "Did Ms. Wick bring her inside to protect her?" she asked.

Will shrugged. "I don't think Jack o' Lantern would have allowed that."

They heard the familiar meow from the cat who knew his name. Where was he?

Buddy searched, too, her ears perked and her furry head darting from side to side. She growled.

Then she yelped and jumped backward.

Had something taken a swipe at her nose?

Something small, and orange, and—invisible?

"Ha!" said Mina, dropping to the floor and waving her hand through the air till she found the furry tabby. "Jacko is invisible! That's how Ms. Wick is protecting him from Buddy!"

Buddy whined and licked her snout in embarrassment.

"Well," said Will, "Witch Wick *did* warn you, Buddy. No dogs allowed."

As he settled back on his heels, he heard something from the corner of the room. *Laughter.* The hairs stood up on the back of his neck. "You know, Ms. Wick might be in here, too," he whispered to Mina.

Her eyes grew wide. "You're right," she said. Then she cleared her throat. "Ms. Wick, if you're in here, I just want you to know—we want to help you. If there's anything you need while you're here . . ."

As her voice trailed off, they heard nothing but silence and the gentle *drip, drip, drip* of raindrops on the roof. The storm was finally passing.

Then Will had an idea.

"We could bring you books!" he said. "Any books you want from the library."

A breeze ruffled his hair, as if someone had suddenly stood up. Then he saw the quill rise from the shelf, poised to take notes. A scrap of paper floated down to the table. And the quill began to scratch back and forth across it.

"She's making a list!" said Mina, turning to him in amazement. "She wants books. We *can* help her!"

Will's insides turned warm as mushroom stew.

Maybe Ms. Wick would never go back to Little Oak. Like Seth's zombie pigmen stepping through the portal into the Nether, she had stepped into a whole new world.

But she can still have her books, thought Will. *And thanks to her, I still have my Buddy.*

He stroked his dog's head and then gazed in amazement as the scrap of paper floated from the table toward Mina's outstretched hand.

"We'll go right now, Ms. Wick," said Mina, jumping up. "The storm has passed. We can be back with the books before dark. Right, Will?"

He nodded and then whispered something in Mina's ear.

"*You* want to stop for *potion* ingredients?" she asked, as if that were the last thing she'd expected to hear come out of his mouth.

Will shrugged. "We're almost out of healing potions," he said. "We're going to need to brew more. I'll help this time."

Mina flashed him the widest smile as she led the way out the door. And Will was pretty sure he heard more laughter from the depths of the witch hut behind him.

As he turned toward where he thought the witch might be standing, he waved goodbye. And whispered, "Thank you."

There really *was* more than one way to fight a battle. And now Will was ready.